CHAPTER 1: SEPTEMBER 28TH, 2018

I lay in bed for a minute, a war going on in my mind. Do I get up or not? It was stupid I know, but one small decision could have changed everything. Provided, I wouldn't have known, but if I went with the leavers departing that day I might not have been writing this. The threats were small at first and not to worry about... Were. You see, when a Mysterious group has a disliking to your, and other people's, governments, it ends in much more then tears, Trust me. As I walked downstairs half awake and lazily grabbed my breakfast, I noticed that there was an announcement on the radio that The Leaver's boats were departing. I knew it would come one day; I mean with a name like The Leavers it was only to be expected anyway. Not many people were on the boat, but it was still obvious that tensions were high and people were itching to get out of England. No one was quite sure when the un named group (that most people had dubbed the name 'The Organization' as people believed it to be one of the largest groups ever formed, with an estimated 1 in 3000 people believed to be linked to the group in some way) was going to strike from the shadows, the government, along with many others had estimated the strike being in 2021, but it was all extremely vague for now.

Late, again. I suppose there was no reason to get to school on time anymore. Same old lessons anyway, I walked straight to the

"I suggest you get your act together young man." He said sternly putting his muffin down. I turned around and walked in the direction of my next lesson, maths.

I sat outside the door for the rest of lunch. I wasn't hungry. I trudged inside the classroom and miserably grabbed my book and sat down in my place. Eventually everyone walked in. I say walk, I mean run. All of them were pushing and shoving in through the door and some were even hitting each other. What's more, Sir didn't even seem to mind. He just sat in his chair finishing his fourth cake. I would have noticed that, if I wasn't trying to stop people from throwing my book across the room. Sir stood up. "Silence…" He mumbled. "Copy the…Date…And." He was cut of mid half-hearted sentence by a flying pencil. He sat down again and started to snore. "Hey look Sir's dead!" Shouted one of the pupils. Everyone started laughing. I stood up and ducked a pencil case. I ran out the door What the hell was going on? I looked down the corridor. Three girls were standing on a table laughing and singing like drunks. I glanced back in the classroom to find Someone running at the window with a chair. I ran outside. It was no better. I saw the Head running around madly and children frantically running around the place laughing and wreaking havoc. I went towards the main building entrance. No point, there were just more children over there. I ran back to the open space. Then I saw it. There was the sudden wail of the fire bell and I could see a fire in one of the buildings. Great I thought, great. I had an Idea. Why don't I run and jump over the fence? Sure, it wasn't a short drop, but I didn't have much of a choice. Then I remembered. James. I started shouting "James, James!" I hoped to god he hadn't eaten any cakes. "James!" I ran around the place screaming, then I stopped and listened for a second. I could hear shouting. Provided, there were lots of people shouting but none of them were using quite as much colourful language than this one. I found where the voice was coming from. "Oh god. The burning!" I ran towards the voice that lead me to a door. Luckily, there was no manic people there, I instantly went for the handle. " Hippity hoppity get off my property." Only one person could make jokes as bad as that. I turned around. It was Scott. "C'mon man, I don't want to fight you." I moaned. Firstly, I didn't have time, Secondly, Scott was a martial arts machine. I heard a window smashing in the background. He started laughing. "I'm going to kill you." he laughed. Now Scott wasn't particularly tall, but his strength made up for that. Scott was not a person to mess with. Whoops. He lunged at me with a strong punch and hit me in the jaw. I backed off clutching my bleeding lip. "That's it. Now you've annoyed me." I kicked him in the stomach and he just kept laughing. "Oh, that's going to hurt like billy-o when you wake up." I winced and ducked a side kick to the hips. I grabbed his leg, but he hit me before I could trip him up. I bent over and started coughing. Scott grabbed my back and shoved me aside. I laid on the floor. My vision blurring. Scott cackled and kicked me over. "If that's how you want to play it." I groaned, standing up. I hit him in the nuts, hard! Sure, it wasn't very imaginative, but it made Scott laugh a little less enthusiastically. I smiled before realising that he was my friend. *He's going to hate me.* I thought before remembering he was the one attacking me. "FOR GODS SAKE HELP!" Screamed James from inside the building. "Sorry gotta scoot." I said to Scott who looked like he was in great pain. I grabbed a hold of the handle and pulled. I was about to step inside when. "What's... going on?" Scott croaked. Could it be? I Looked at him. "HAHAHA." My heart sank. He was holding a massive metal bench. I dived out the way as he threw it in my direction. The bench made a huge dent in the large metal wall. How the hell could he do that? I ran at him ready to push him over but to no avail. He kneed me in the side and I fell onto a bench. In those brief seconds I thought. I'm faster than Scott. Then I ran through the door and to where the screaming was coming from. He was following me laughing. Pain enveloped my body, but I didn't care. I had to make it.

I found James in a science classroom that was starting to catch flames. James was dragging a dazed Arran out from under the desk. "Took your time!" Said James. "Wait, why was he here?" I

5

said, "Arran said that he was going to go the see his Form Tutor as he didn't feel well. Look we don't have much time here!" James said. I looked around. "Oh great." Scott was at the end of the corridor, wiping blood from his mouth and grimacing. I ran back inside the science classroom. I could hear James shouting, but I didn't care. I was looking for one thing. I filled a tray full of water and put it aside. Then I grabbed as many harmful metals in strange looking vials as I could. I heard shouting from outside. Sounded like Scott was getting close. I grabbed the tray and metals and dived out the door shoving James out the way. I slid the tray towards Scott. "RUN!" I shouted. James started to drag Arran towards the lift. I threw all the metals in the tray. "Skidoo Skiday"-BOOM. I ran as fast as I could and leapt into the lift with James and Arran just as the doors were drawing to a close.

CHAPTER 3: SEPTEMBER 29TH, 2018

W e sat in a circle in the clearing all huddled round the phone like penguins keeping warm. "So, we can trace the call to the recipient's phone?" I inquired. "A bit more complicated but basically...yes. To put it in its most watered-down term." Arran had thought it up, he had seen it somewhere on a cop film. He didn't know how but we managed to piece it together with the help of James being a tech nerd. We had to install a few dodgy apps and put a little too much money on the poor man's bank account, but it was all for a perfectly good course and none of us really cared any way. "So, you say that this is your sisters' number?" Said James. "Yes...I think so..." I replied. I was rubbish with phone numbers. "This should be fun." said Arran. He had fully recovered but didn't get much sleep because 'I snore'. "So, the instant we press this button, either this phone will get a virus, or hopefully it will work." We were all in anticipation over calling my sister. I would laugh if I was in the mood. He pressed the button. The annoying phone call noise sounded across the small clearing. "Great." Said Arran. "Turn it off before a crank hears, quick!" I yelled. Looking slightly embarrassed, James put the phone on silent and got over 100 notifications, including one that said 'system U isn't responding' James swiped down. "Well this is easy." 'My home address popped up. "Hey that's my house!" I exclaimed sarcastically. "Well done Sherlock." Muttered

Arran. We climbed the hill and bid farewell to the alcove and our sanity. It was 5 O'clock in the morning when we left, all the cranks would be asleep by then... hopefully. It was when we jumped over the barrier and into the dog walking route that we realised it was incredibly dark. Arran turned on the torch on the phone, it wasted the battery sure but at least we didn't have to squint at everything. It was eerie in the dark, especially with an apocalyptic vibe to everything. We had a plan, but nothing could prepare us for what happened next. "and that was how I got this scar." Said Arran but was shortly cut off by the sound of Laughing. We all stopped in are tracks. Arran dropped the phone into a bush out of shock. "Well done you." Complained James. The laughing got louder. And louder We hid in a bush. The sound was coming from the top of the bridge and seemed to be making its way down the slope at the side. We listened. The laughing became even louder. There was a scrambling noise as the thing tripped down the slope. We could barely see the dark silhouette of a person. I grabbed a branch. "Ready for round two." Whispered Arran. " Hey, anyone got the internet code?" We freezed on the spot. I picked up the phone and shone it at the thing. "Oi watch where your pointing that!" Dylan said. "Wait. What are you doing here?" Sure enough a grubby Dylan with twigs in his hair was standing there, illuminated by the light ."We could ask you the same thing." Replied James. "Nice to see you too." He muttered. "We were just on our way to pick up my sister..." I said. "And you?" "Well... I have been here a few times with Chris and it was the first place I thought of going, after Tesco." He started but was cut off by Arran. "Did you eat any food after the outbreak?" I was rather abrupt, but Dylan was used to this. "No...it all smelt funny." He said, accompanied by sighs from the trio. "Got any supplies?" was the first thing that came to James's mind. "I have my conduct card." He replied. "Gotta keep it on you at all times!" We stared at him, were we dreaming? "So are you coming with us or not?" I took him a while to consider this, so I said, "We have flappy bird on this phone?" He grinned. "Well I can't refuse now." It only took us a few minutes to get to the end of the path, phone torch in hand. Maybe because the atmosphere was a little lighter. Shame Scott wasn't here. I felt guilty for a second then realised that Scott was the strongest out of all of us. "Where are the other boys?" I asked as we reached the end of the route. "Umm... I kind of lost them..." He said. "Like turned into cranks or just lost?" I said. He frowned. " Isn't that from the Maze Runner?" He asked. We all looked at Arran he grinned smugly. "Yes. Yes, it is." It was only a short walk now, down my small road. We all kept our eyes peeled. There were lots of houses round here. More houses equal more people equals more cranks. There was the occasional bark from a dog, but nothing drastic. And then I saw it. "Here it is." I said, holding back tears. The glass windows were all smashed, and the front door bashed off its hinges. Arran patted me on the back. I smiled. At least I still had my friends and hopefully Emily. All the lights in the house were on so we turned the phone light off. We stood outside the door. "So, when we get in there, Arran takes the living room, James takes the study and Dylan takes the conservatory." I said. "I will take the upstairs." I smiled. I knew where Emily would be. We stepped over the threshold and into the house. The place was a tip. Lego could be found in every corner of the place; the banister was ripped to shreds and the computers were missing. "Who could've done this?" Dylan whispered. "I don't want to know." Replied James. I went upstairs. Every floorboard creaking as I stepped on it. I paused. A shiver going down my spine. "Huston, we have a problem." I said. I glanced up the stairs and sure enough there was Emily. I would have been happy if-"HAHAHAHAH!" "RUN!" I screamed I dashed down the stairs "Behind the table!" I yelled. We all darted behind the dining table, hearts racing. "Where are you?" Emily cackled. Crank Emily cackled. "This isn't going to be easy." I whispered. " Does your sister always act like this?" Dylan exclaimed. I peeked from behind the table. Emily was in the living room with a sickly grin on her face. "Well you going to do it or not?" Whispered James. I braced myself, this wasn't going to be easy. I Cracked my knuckles. I stood up and slid over the table, sending the mats and the plant pot flying everywhere. Emily turned around; eyes ablaze. I ran into the living room and pushed her onto the sofa. Sorry, this is gonna hurt." I said and hit her in the face. I winced. Emily lay there, dazed. I stood up. "What the hell just happened?" I heard from behind the table. "We need biscuit ketchup, anything you can find." I said. Arran grabbed the biscuits off the table and threw them at me. Dylan looked in the fridge and pulled what was left of it out. Every cupboard was opened, and food thrown at me. I looked at the side. The blender was still there. I sighed. After blending everything together, I put it in a jug. "She's going to hate me." I said. I went over to her and started to pour the horrible mixture into her mouth. "Let's hope that the poison cancels itself out." I stood there, admiring my handywork. "When she wakes up, she will either be a Crank or an Emily. I went back to the table. "What do we do now?" Asked James. "I don't know to be honest, but we need some more food…" I said. "Right, I will go to the farm with James, Arran and Dylan you look over Emily. Be ready for when she wakes up, she has a terrible temper. After she wakes up call us on the phone, seeing the battery is so low we will have the phone shut down until…" I glanced at my watch. "6:30, Ok?" They all nodded. James stood up and walked over to me. "Now we just need to pack a few stuffs and we'll be off." I looked at the shed. I had an idea. We left the house on bike with back packs filled with poisoned food in it. You never know. It was getting slightly lighter and we couldn't find a power pack, so we were all slightly upset. We cycled down our road, me leading. At the end of our road there was a small farm. "We'll go to the farm; the Organisation can't poison our animal produce. We heard laughing in the background somewhere. It didn't matter. If anything it made us cycle faster. "Over there." I said, pointing ahead. There was a small cycle route leading up to a woods. "We can access the farm from here I'm pretty sure." We turned our bikes in. Everything was going to plan until the laughing started. And didn't stop.

CHAPTER 4: KLEPTOPARASITES

We froze in our tracks, the farm just a few meters away from us. "What do we do now?" James asked. We didn't have many options. I looked around. " I say we get the food and force it down his throat." I said. James looked confused. "And then he lets us steal his produce." He replied. I scowled at him. It was a good point though. "You really want another fight?" I said to him, the laughing growing louder. "Go get the food." James said, staring at the machinery. "I have other plans." We jumped over the poorly built fence and put our bags to aside. The farmer had spotted us. His hair (What was left of it) was almost as wild as his eyes. He looked straight at us laughing. Then he ran. "Go!" Shouted James. I ran over to the chicken coop There should be eggs there. I rushed over. It was a metal chicken coop that required a key. I groaned before realising that the gaps were big enough to fit Connors ego through. I reached in and grabbed as many eggs as I could. Then I remembered. This was the easy part. The mad farmer was too close for my liking. I heard the hum of a big machine. I didn't look round. I looked around furiously. It was cold and wet, and I was hungry. Perfect. I looked about, there was a churn of milk. It was too big to carry. I moaned but was cut off by a hand reaching my shoulder. I looked behind me. "Hello." Said the farmer. He hit me in the stomach and I went flying. No. Literally. I landed some half a meter off. How could an old man like that be so powerful? Like Scott I remembered. "Get out the way!" screamed James I Couldn't see him anywhere. I jumped up and scrambled to the fence. Then I saw him, or more like a huge combine harvester "How the hell did you get in one of those?" I yelled at him. There was no reply as the huge thing tumbled across the grass, the massive blades crunched across the path it was making. "You should really take care of your machine keys more!" He shouted as the thing trundled past. The man stopped smiling. He took a long, hard think and then ran the opposite way. He jumped into the sheep pen and started pushing them out the way as he ran. "Ha-ha!" James laughed. He pulled the joystick. Again. And again. He stopped smiling. "Umm... Is it supposed to do this?" He asked. I stood there in terror. "Jump! I said. He didn't hear me. "Jump!" He started to go pale. The machine was inches away from the sheep pen, the animals quite contently eating grass. "You know what?" James said, voice wobbling. "I'm going to jump." "Probably a good idea." I mumbled. He stood up on the steps, face grey. He gulped. The machine was inches away. He jumped and landed without any ceremony on the ground. I glanced at the sheep pen. The fence was being trampled on and the sheep were being displaced everywhere. I looked back at James. He stared at me in horror from the floor as the sound of bleating and machine cogs crunching filled the early morning. I winced. "Whoops..." Said James slowly. Ignoring the horrible crunching sound I walked over to the milk churn and picked it up. "Going to put the eggs in the bag." James said. I stood there, thinking of ways to carry this thing. "Hey..." James said. "We seem to have 5 Missed calls..." I ran over to him. "We got to get this thing on fast!" The sun was rising, and the Cranks seemed to be awake. Just what we needed. I found a long piece of rope in a bush lining the fence. "You're going to have to drop that." I said, pointing to my bag. It was only food any way. I grabbed the churn and tied it to my back with the rope. "C'mon!" I said we both sat on our bike and pushed off the ground. We cycled back to my house at a rate of knots. Looking around every so often to check there were no cranks. We only encountered two. We were lucky. The first one tried to grab

James's bag and the second just ran after us shouting "YOU CAN'T CATCH ME I'M THE GINGERBREAD MAN!" The sun was getting way to high and the temperature was rising. Things only got worse when we got back to my house. We found a crank at the door trying to get in, but Arran and Dylan were on the other side pushing the de-hinged door up to its frame. James got off his bike halfway down the drive, but I didn't I was going too fast to waste this opportunity. The crank looked round confused before I leapt off my bike and threw my weight on it. I hoped it was the milk churn that knocked it out cold, and not me. The door was put to aside and I was helped up by "Emily?" She was fully recovered and looked slightly grumpy. "Please don't pour disgusting smoothies down my throat again what the hell.". I heard laughing. "Come on, no time for family reunions." Said Arran. Me and James walked in with our supplies and Arran, Dylan and Emily put the door back. "Made any progress?" I said. "Well I've given Scruff enough biscuits to last this whole thing over." Said Emily. I looked at Arran and Dylan. "Well..." Began Dylan. "We found a suitable phone and some walkie-talkies and also made more anti-crank mix." Finished Arran. "And found Fortnite mobile." Said Dylan. "Great." I replied. Now shove every useful thing in a pile in the living room, we will share it between 5 back packs." The three got busy to work. I turned to Emily. "So...what have you been doing for the day?" I said, trying to make polite conversation. "Well, I ate a brownie and next thing I know I am singing all-star and going to feed the cat." She said. "Did you bump into Mum and Dad?" I asked hopefully. "No." She replied, sighing. I frowned in confusion and the went into the living room and sighed. "Essentials only."

When I was done, about half the pile was gone and I heard more laughing. I rushed to the study and over to the study window. I looked suspiciously through the blinds. 5 cranks were wandering the streets. We poured the milk into 6 water bottles, one for Ronnie and sat down to eat badly made boiled eggs. "What are you looking at me for? It was Dylan who made them." I said. "Well could you do a better job?" He replied. "We need to get moving said Emily from the study. We all got to work packing our bags and getting bikes out of the shed when it occurred to me. How are we going to get a bike up to Ronnie? Everyone looked at me and Arran "I didn't know we were getting Ronnie." I sighed. "We will think about it once we have got him." I said. Arran, Dylan and Emily had pushed their bikes to the front of the back gate. Everything was set. "Ready?" I said. "It's not going to be easy; everyone follow Arran, he apparently knows where he's going." Arran smiled smugly. We opened the gate. There were still a few cranks, but they didn't see us. Me and James grabbed our bikes and we all rode our bikes up to the end of the driveway. There were at least 10 Cranks to the left of us. We smiled at each other. "Ronnie better be grateful." Emily muttered. "Going all the way up to Estuary View." And with that we cycled off. A trail of laughter behind us.

CHAPTER 5: THE SPLIT

We had only cycled a few meters when. "Ryan, should there be 1ten cranks following us?" I looked around and sure enough, ten cranks were on our tail, laughing like hyenas. "Umm… probably not…" I replied. We hadn't even got to the end of my road yet. "Perfect" Muttered Arran. We were cycling at a pace faster than them, but they seemed to get closer by the second. "What do we do now?" Emily said panting. I considered our options. We still had a long way to go and we couldn't keep up the speed the whole way around, especially on small roads like this. "Someone open their bag." I said. We didn't have much of a choice. "What!" Said James! "Just do it." I replied, the cranks gaining on us. "Here goes nothing!" Said Dylan. He reached behind him, opened the bag and threw it on the floor. Slowly, stuff started to pour out of it. The cranks behind us looked nothing more than slightly disturbed. "Well done!" James shouted. "Oi it wasn't me who opened the bag!" I screamed back. "Will you guys stop!" Said Emily. The place fell silent apart from the sound of laughing. "Down here." Said Arran in front. We had come to a roundabout. I gritted my teeth. This wasn't going to be easy. "Turn here." He said, going around it. I braced myself and started to cycle on it. There was a bunch of trees in the middle. I glanced behind; the cranks were stepping onto it. "What are you doing?" Shouted Dylan I was inches away and then I skidded out the way as fast as I could. A few cranks followed pursuit but most of them hit the trees and were stopped in their tracks. No time to celebrate. I thought I bumped off the roundabout and joined the rest.

James's face was thunder. "Hey what's up?" I grinned turning off down the Thanet way. Usually, this place would be crawling with cars, but I could only see one car. Following us. "Hey guys…" I said. "Not in the mood." Said James. "Well sorry!" I replied. Dylan turned around. "It was your idea about the bag mate!" I was beginning to get annoyed. "Shouting at me is" SCRREECH. I was cut off by the car that was getting way too close to be safe. "Look where we are now." Dylan said. "Will you shut up!" Cried Emily. She was right. It was childish, but I didn't care. I spat at Dylan's bike. Arran turned around. "Oh God Ryan, GO GO GO" I cycled as fast as I could even the cranks were still following us. "Screw you!" I screamed. "If it weren't for me you two wouldn't be a-" The car bumped into me as lightly as it could, but it was still a jolt. "YOU MIND!" I yelled. And what I did next should not be done at home. I cycled to the side of the car and pulled my bike breaks. I saw the car speeding past, the cranks reaching out the window I jolted forwards. I reached out to the car, my hands sliding across the back off it. I managed to get a hold on something and pulled myself onto the back of the car. I stood up slowly wobbling through the car speed. I looked down a crank that looked extremely like my Uncle started to hit the window. I crawled onto the roof of the car and felt the roof vibrate from the loud rap music they were playing. It was extremely tasteless as well. I cringed for a second then thought of something, I was still wearing my backpack. I put it down on the roof and grabbed my old phone that was in there. I tried to turn it on. No battery as usual. I hit it against the front driver's window. It smashed into pieces I looked at my phone. Not a scratch. Good old big phones I thought. I got the anti-crank mix out of my mix out of my bag. This will be fun. I leant down and squirted the mix into the drivers face. He spluttered, and the car started swerving all over the place. It was going towards the edge of the road and into a fence, Just as I planned. The car crashed, sending my uncle flying out the open window. I got thrown forward sliding off the front bonnet. Arran and the others were well behind me. I stood up at the side of the road. It was only a bush and the car generally looked ok. Everyone inside was knocked out. I looked at the car and then to the bikes. And then back to the car. Why not? I thought I climbed in through the window. Turn left Said the sat nav. "No thanks." I said Climbing into the driver's seat. I knew my way from here. I looked at the steering wheel. How hard could it be? I thought. I pressed on the gas and pulled the car out the side of the road. I looked at the gear stick. Looks boring I thought before driving like a drunk driver down the road. It was wobbly at first, but I got used to it after a while. Turn left. Said the sat nav a little sterner. I looked in the wing mirror. James was sticking his middle finger up at me. Concentrate on the road I thought. Only a little way now. The cranks beside me looked familiar. I frowned. Auntie Excel? Leo? Truth dawned. I just threw my aunt out the window. I gulped. Whoops. Turn left. "Look can you shut up please!" I said. Stop navigation to... Disneyland? "Yes yes yes!" I yelled. Locating to...Yeshiva student accommodation centre. It replied "NO!" I sighed. And rolled my eyes. Something I should not have done. There was another round about coming up. I skidded to a side, narrowly missing it but instead started to move towards the building next to it. 'Playing 'No' by Meghan.' I opened the door and leapt out just as the car crashed into the stairs leading up to the place. I lay on the steps coughing. I looked at the car. It had bashed into the stairs and was smoking. Where am I? I thought I sat up. And looked around. There was a grassy hill about 5 meters tall and a concrete path going up it with a metal handrail. I looked up further. Sitting on the hill was the hospital. I sighed. I had made it. I. Where were the others? I was going to look down the road but heard laughing close to me. I dived for a bush. I peeked out from behind it. 2 cranks were roaming around drinking something alcoholic. 3 more cranks appeared to my left smashing everything in their path with a "Motor bike?" Then it hit me, they must have super strength like Scott and the psychopathic farmer. I looked back to the estuary view. It looked like the most undamaged place in the whole area. Ronnie is in the middle of that Somewhere I thought. Poor bloke. He must be starving. Or a crank the other half of my brain said. This could be dangerous. Very dangerous. I heard shouting and looked around wildly. From my spot in the hedge I could quite clearly see Dylan, James, Arran and Emily fighting off the two drunks. I slowly walked out from behind the hedge. It looked dangerous. I stayed there for a moment as the last one got finished off by Emily. "Hey... Ummm... Pretty close one there..." I said walking closer towards them. They were in the middle of the road scowling at me. "Like you can talk." Said James "Ow!" I yelled. A rock bounced off my shoulder. "You could have given us a lift!" Said Arran. I looked at him. "Sorry mate! Every man for himself, this is a war!" I yelled getting cross. "We are your friends for god's sake, not your slaves!" Said James. "Look, this is getting petty now! We need all the people we can get!" Dylan scowled at Emily. "The lizard doesn't count as a person, get rid of that." He said. Emily lunged at him. "YOU WATCH WHAT YOUR SAYING IDIOT!" She shouted. He tried to hit her. "Come on Dylan." Said Arran beckoning him over to them. "She's not worth your energy." He stated. "But he is." Replied James staring at me. "Look what did I." I started but was cut off by I kick in the knee. I walked back, clutching my leg in pain. I stood there for a second. Motionless. Dylan advanced forward "Ryan..." He started. I leapt towards him and hit him in the chin. He backed off. "Idiot." He muttered. James and Arran started to walk off "Come on Dylan, don't bother a genius." He said to him glaring at me. "Look, if it weren't for me you would be dead, I saved you! I found you Dylan! You have all eaten the eggs that I have..." I stopped. They didn't turn around just kept on walking. They grabbed their bikes. "You stay away from my lizard!" Yelled Emily at the boys. Arran and Dylan cycled off down the road. James stayed. He spat at my feet. "Every man for himself." He said before cycling off leaving me and Emily alone. I started to run after them shouting. They didn't turn around. My best friends, gone. What have I done I thought? What have I done?

CHAPTER 6: WAKE UP

I turned to Emily. She was scowling, looking at the road. "How dare he." She muttered. I sat on the curb, head in hands. "Great team this is. Great team." Emily sat down next to me. "Sitting here isn't going to find Ronnie." She said. True. "Think of all the people we've lost." I said sighing. Emily looked into the distance. I counted them, one by one. The boys. Scott, Mum, Dad, James, Arran, Dylan. I was holding back tears. Don't cry I thought. This is your fault. I stood up, taking Emily by surprise. "Come on." I said sniffing. "Let's find him." We walked up the concrete steps up to the building. "For them." I said. "For them." Said Emily. We opened the door. The lobby was... Erie. The T.V was smashed, and the place was way too quiet. Me and Emily snuck in. "I would call Ronnie on the phone if I had his number." I shook my head and looked at the floor. I didn't see him as often as the others. Emily beckoned me over. Tucked away at the side there was a lift. I walked over, and she pressed the button. PING. The doors opened." It's too quiet." Said Emily. I glanced around. This was too easy. The lift doors opened slowly. It was the only few second I hadn't spent running the whole day. And I hated it. We stepped into the lift. "What button do we press?" Emily asked. I thought for a second. "Top floor is for severe injuries; Ronnie had a massive gash down his face." Emily pressed the button to the top floor. The lift doors closed. "Wait, since when did this thing have music in it?" I turned around. No one was there I sighed. The atmosphere was dark and uneasy. I could see Emily was on edge too by the look on her face. I turned towards the lift doors. PING. The doors opened. This floor was virtually tidy as well. Something was wrong. "We should go back." Whispered Emily. "Agreed" I replied, breathing heavy. We went towards the lift and pressed the button. Then. "Turn around." Said a crackly voice that must have been edited by a voice changer. A chill went down my spine. I turned around slowly. There was nothing. I looked all over the place. Nothing. Then it hit me. It was coming out the T.V. Where's Ronnie. I said sternly. "He's fine. More than fine. He's practically laughing. don't worry." Replied the T.V. "You maniac!" Said Emily. I swore at him. "So It's you, you're the organisation!" I was going red. I hit the T.V on the wall. "Not just me." Said the T.V a little way down the corridor. It cackled. "The whole of England now!" It replied. I looked at Emily, she was going white. "You never see past the adventure Ryan, It's your downfall." Emily started to back up against the wall. "You idiot. I control the…" "Crank?" Said Arran I looked around wildly. Only Emily was there. It was driving me mad. "I've been watching you." Observing your every move through the CCTV cameras. You really need to improve your security more." The voice sounded cocky. He only added to my list of people to hit. "You know." The voice began. "Shut up." I said quite calmly. "What? The voice inquired. "Shut up." I replied a little more sternly. "You're a bully. I know how to deal with them. You're just a sad little man behind a computer. You're a coward trying to be like the cool kids. Pathetic." I said directly into the nearest CCTV camera. "Defiantly the leader of the group I can" "We will find you." Started Emily standing up straight. "And when we do we will give you massive dose of anti-crank mix. Mark my words." I looked at her, smiling. A crank burst through the door to the left of me. "Time for you to meet your end." The voice said. I kept starring at the camera. Another one crawled through the elevator doors. "And when we find you." I said, two others bashing out the vent. "You will wish that you had never even started this." I continued. The T.V speakers went static and the cranks closed in. "Get off!" Yelled Emily I spun around. There were cranks everywhere. I thought about jumping out the window but 1: The way was crowded with cranks and 2: I couldn't lose another friend. My mind was crowded. For the first time in a day I actually felt scared. I looked around wildly. The cranks were inches away laughing. "RYAN!" Screamed Emily I couldn't see her. I spun around on the spot. "Who could've done this?" Said Dylan I yelled, thrashing out wildly. I was breathing heavy. I could feel the musty smell of a crank's breath on my back. I couldn't think straight. I got hit in the head hard. I fell on the floor, my vision blurring. "Bad dream?" Said an imaginary James. I was starting to go cold; I was being dragged off by the cranks. My eyes started to close, the words echoing round my head and then I gave into the embrace of the blackness. I was floating in and out of consciousness. Do I get up or not? I was laying in my bed, everything blurry. I tried to sit up, I couldn't, it was like I was being held down. There was a voice in the background, indistinguishable. I yanked my arms up and tried my best to sit up, I couldn't I pushed and pushed. I was stuck. People started to rush past me. I managed to spot Scott, Ronnie, Dad and Emily. I was strapped to the bed. "Wake up said Arran." I was hazy. I tugged some more, fading, drifting. Light. I was sweating profusely. I observed my surroundings. I was in the back of a van. We were in the back of a van. I relaxed a bit. Emily was still here. I tugged at my arms and legs. I was tied up. Emily was still asleep, and I could see a small lizard crawling across the place. The driving was bad and made me feel sick. Cranks no doubt. I realised that I was tied to a wooden board. Great start. I still had a phone in my pocket, on further inspection I realised it was my sisters' phone. She's going to hate me. I thought for the second time today. I didn't know what time it was, but the van was light because of a lantern in the corner. Maintenance van? Any way, we needed to get out of here fast and alive preferably. I shuffled as much as I could being tied to a wooden board over to Emily and started to whisper to her. "Come on Emily, wake up!" It had no effect. "Come on!" I whispered. The car jolted to a stop. I was plunged forwards. I heard the doors open and the close briefly after. "Here we go!" I thought. The sound of boots on tarmac filled the night and was followed by laughter. "What do we do now?" Asked Arran. I looked around, no one there. I heard the doors opening and closed my eyes and acted like I was in a deep sleep. The person/people didn't speak at all. They started to unstrap me. I was ready. I leapt up, kicking ahead of me, managing to hit someone. I dashed out the van. That should wake Emily up. I started running. I was on a road near my house and It was incredibly dark. I looked at my watch. Darn. I had missed 00:00 by 20 minutes. I pulled out the phone and put flashlight mode on to see where I was going. It looked like straight tarmac basically with a deep ditch at the side a few meters off. It'll do I thought. I ran towards that. I heard people running after me. I didn't want to go through this again. I kept on running. I dived into the ditch. It was deep enough to hide a person. Lucky me. The cranks were getting closer and closer. I braced myself for a fight. "It's us Ryan!" said one of them. I didn't look up. Scott tried this trick. "Come on Idiot." Said another. I smiled only one person said that. "Arran?" I whispered. I stood up slowly and none the less there was Arran standing there. I looked some more and saw James, Dylan and "Long time no see." Said Ronnie. I got out of the ditch. "But how?"

CHAPTER 7: ONE MAN'S TRASH, ANOTHER MAN'S TREASURE

James:

"**I**diot." I muttered while cycling away on my bike trying to catch up with the others. He has common sense; he and Emily will come with us on their bikes any second now. I could hear Arran and Dylan having a conversation that was less than polite ahead as well. I caught them up. "Where do we go now?" Arran asked. I paused before saying "I say we go back to the alcove; it'll be night soon." We were all fed up. I mean sure, it was us that ditched Ryan, but it was him that ditched us first. I could tell that that was exactly what the other 2 were thinking as they were frowning. "We'll take a short cut to avoid any cranks." Said Arran and was the only thing that was said for ages. The route was much longer and took us up to at least 7:20 but at least we didn't run into any laughing trouble. We ended up at the start of the cycle route and I think we all sighed at the prospect of resting for a few precious minutes. When we reached the barrier we put our bikes outside because cycling them up there was too much for today. We leapt over the barrier one by one and trudged down the muddy path with our back packs until we reached the place. We rolled down the hill and sat down on the floor. There was a long silence until Dylan said. "Hey, why is Lucas lift pass here?" We didn't reply. We weren't in the mood as Ryan would say. That reminded me, they weren't here yet. What was going on? "Hey, I'm going to call Ryan. He and Emily should be here by now." I said Arran and Dylan grumbled but I think they both agreed. I brought out the old man's phone and dialled Emily's number. I didn't know his number and he didn't have his phone on him anyway, it was his Sisters. I phoned it. No reply. I got a handful of notifications. "Oh go away!" I said and deleted them. I phoned again. We were all sitting in a circle in anticipation. "Hey…do you think he's…Ok?" He asked with a hint of concern in his voice. I got more notifications. "Before you swipe away check them, just to be sure." Arran said. I sighed and looked at them. I frowned. "He's gone from the estuary and is traveling to Clowes woods, the woods at the end of the farm. "Maybe he's lost?" Said Dylan. After that we had a long argument about who should go to find him. "Fine." Said Arran "I'll go." The instant he left the alcove the atmosphere got darker. To ward it off me and Dylan passed the time talking about what we had done before we met each other at the bridge. We laughed occasionally. "Now it's your turn." I said to Dylan. He paused for a second. "Well, basically after the fight with the year 11's I went to music and things started to go hay wire from there. I ran straight out the entrance and made my way to the first place I thought of which just happened to be Tesco. There were lots of people there, so I snuck in the back exit as it was open and hid in a staff only place playing with all the toys in stock until night-time. Then I went into the main store to." He was mid-way through quite a strange story when Arran tumbled into the alcove, face pale. "Guys…Ryan and Emily are being dragged up the woods by cranks." We all starred at him for a moment. "We leave him for one second!" I exclaimed. "They are unconscious by the looks of things, so we are going to need a van and fast!" We all got to work packing our stuff and walking down the path. "How are we going to get a van?" Dylan said. "We'll get the closest van we see that has it's keys in it." I said. "That's my kind of plan!" Said Arran. We jumped over the barrier and grabbed our bikes. It only took us a second this time to reach the end of the cycle route. It was starting to get cold and dark; I could see that Dylan was regretting signing up for this. Especially during what happened next. It only took a bit of cycling. "There's your van." Said Arran. Me and Dylan looked over to where he was pointing and saw a van playing the Wii theme tune at full blast . I couldn't see any cranks in the front, so they must all be in the back. "Do we have to?" Moaned Dylan. We cycled as close to the van as we could before parking our bikes, we would need them later. We crept up to van with anti-crank mix and the anything that we found in our back packs that might be useful against happy zombies. "Ready?" I had to shout over the loud music. I opened the doors and was met with sight of 2 cranks dancing to Wii music like drunk idiot I leapt in the car and hit 1 in the stomach. "Ow..." He laughed. Dylan got the other one. We chucked them out the car, they were too drunk to do anything, so they just lay there on the floor laughing. We grabbed our bikes and threw them in the back. The keys were in the ignition. "Right, who's going to drive this thing?" Arran asked. "Me, I know the way up there." It was only a short drive until we had to stop at the entrance and grab our bikes out of the boot. "Right." I said when everyone got their bikes out of the back. "It's not going to be an easy cycle up there, and an even harder one on the way back, so brace yourselves. I will lead with the phone, so we know where we are going. Ready?" Everyone nodded, and Arran mumbled as usual. We pushed our bikes through the entrance and got on them as soon as we could. "Hey, why is there loads of dead sheep in this field?" Dylan asked. "I don't know... strange... umm come on we don't have much time." I said. It wasn't long before we reached a bridge going over the motor way. It was a small trek up there, but nothing compared to what was coming up next. We looked down the motor way. It was completely empty. A shiver went down my spine. "I hate this." Said Arran. I agreed with him. For such a busy city it was wrong to have so little people. We continued cycling down the bridge. I looked ahead. Great. This hill again. I thought. I braced myself and cycled up the hill as fast as I could. Eventually we all made it to the top, panting. I got the phone out of my pocket and called

Emily's number. I looked at the notifications. "It looks like they're walking towards the lake, come on!" We got back on our bikes and cycled off. This part was a bit easier, we made it up to the lake in about 10 minutes. I got off my bike and placing it carefully on the ground and walking up to the ring of trees that surrounded the small clearing around the lake. To my surprise, I could see Will, Luca, Olly, Finn, Ronnie and Lewis in the middle, dragging Emily and Ryan towards the fence lining the pond on two wooden boards. "Great." Muttered Arran. "So we all charge at the cranks and knock them out. Sound like a good plan?" I said. No one replied. We slowly crept up the pathway, towards the cranks, trying not to make any loud noises. I mimed counting 'I,2,3' and then yelled. "RUN!" We all ran at the cranks, arms flailing screaming like in a fantasy book where there is a big battle. I was fighting Finn, who seemed to be tiered and extremely annoyed. "Sorry about this." I said knowing full well that they wouldn't forgive me. I hit him in the nuts hit him in the stomach and threw him in the pond. I looked over at Dylan and Arran. Arran was hitting the crank a few too many times in the face and Dylan was trying to make polite conversation with his as he hit him every time that the crank lunged at him. Where are the other cranks? I thought I looked around and saw them trying to drown Emily and Ryan. "No thanks!" I said and rushed at them. I wrestled them off the boards and shoved them aside. The boards smacked onto the pond bank and I started to drag them off. I got quite a decent distance when one of the cranks grabbed a hold of then boards. It was Ronnie. "But, what?" I said as he laughed and started to pull the boards back. I ran over to the back packs that we had dropped as fast as I could, pulling everything out of it until I found it, the anti-crank mix. I rushed back to Ronnie who was pulling the boards towards the pond and gave him a good dose of the mix watching him spit and splutter as I poured it down his throat. I had never seen a transformation while conscious. It wasn't pretty. Ronnie spluttered and coughed, stumbling back. He fell on the floor. There was a long pause. I walked over to him and reached my hand out and then. "The hell you have to go do that for you ugly child!" He shouted. I smiled. There he was, sure with a several stiches down his face but Ronnie was back.

CHAPTER 8: CAMPFIRE TALES

"Nice to see you." I said, "Why you do that!" He shouted. "And, where am I? I this a prank or something, I don't get it." "Follow me." I said. "Why is Ryan Emily strapped to boards? Is this some kind of cult Jesus?" I picked up the boards and went over to Arran and Dylan, they had finished off the cranks. "Ronnie!" Shouted Arran and Dylan "You're in the cult too? And you didn't let me into this stuff. Well thanks a lot kids." He said. "Now we need to get these 2 down tom the van, come on!" Arran started to unstrap them. "Wait." I said, the boards could come in handy." Everyone looked at me confused, especially Ronnie. "Bear with me." I said and started to grab Emily's board. I dragged it down the small pathway and out of the alcove. I then proceeded to push her board down the hill. It slid a bit slow but then caught up speed. I looked at Arran, Dylan and Ronnie. They stared at me in horror. "Seems fun." Said Dylan and then proceeded to grab Ryan's board and follow pursuit. They slid down the hill quite fast. I grabbed my bike and started to cycle after them. The others did the same, apart from Ronnie had to run alongside us. The cycle was a bit easier as everything was downhill. We talked and laughed all the way down I was happy; the team was together again apart from Scott who Ryan sort of blew up with chemicals. I looked at Ronnie running behind us. We had a lot to explain to him. A lot. It wasn't long before we reached the hill. The boards slowed down and stopped at the flat bit before the bridge. I got of my bike and waited for the others. "Drop your bikes." I said. "We won't be able to get up there with everything. 2

people aboard." I said. Arran and Dylan took one board and me and Ronnie took the other. "Hey, is there supposed to be a lizard on this board?" Asked Arran. I looked over; we were halfway up the hill. "I don't see why not?" I said, and we continued walking. Ronnie asked me a lot of questions, but the answer was always the same I'll tell you in the van. It was a long and tiring walk up to the van, but we made it. The hard part was getting the boards past the entrance. We had to stop for a while to do that. But we eventually got them in the back of the van. We all had to squeeze into the front with a lot of complaining from Dylan. "Right." I said." Now I can explain." We drove around the block for a bit talking all about our adventure whilst Ronnie listened in shock horror and admiration. "Is this a dream?" He asked. "Not last time I checked." I replied. "Talking about dreams, it seems like Emily or Ryan are having a bad one in the back." Said Arran. "And that was how we got here." Said James I was sort of glad that the story had ended, it was starting to drag on a bit. "That was a chapter and a half." Said Emily. "No, it was actually a chapter and 560 words." Muttered Arran. "Really!" Said Dylan. "Yeah, count it, oop, now it's a chapter and 575 words." I shrugged it off as an Arran joke and continued with the conversation. We were all sat on the road having a conversation. Not the best place to sit as they drill into you at nursery but who really cared. No one drove on this road any way. We were at outside the van. Me and Dylan were sitting in the van. Instead of a campfire we had the lantern. It was perfect. It wasn't a big fancy amazing fire, but it did virtually the same thing just like our rag tag gang at the end of existence making meme references. Arran showed us his 'massive' scar and we talked the night away and then. "Hey, do you remember anything before you were knocked out.?" Said Ronnie. I took a long think. A long think. "I remember everything before walking into the estuary but there is a long gap of lost memory between that and waking up tied to a board in a van in the middle of nowhere at night." Everyone was deep in thought. "You remember anything Emily?" Ronnie said. "Well I can remember walking into the lift, it was really creepy, and the place was clean, not broken up." We all paused. "Why don't we go back there to jog your memory?" Said James. "No." I said abruptly. James was taken aback. "Sorry, I just have bad non-memories at that place." Everyone looked confused and the atmosphere was much quieter. "Sorry for offending your lizard." "True." I paused. "Sorry for being an idiot." I said. "The war was getting to me. "That's Ok." said James. I smiled. "There's no I in team." I replied. "But there is a meme in memento!" Exclaimed Arran. Only Ronnie laughed to break the silence. "Well." I said looking at my watch. "We best get moving." We all stood up. Dylan put the lantern back in the van and Emily insisted in driving seeing she was the oldest. Ronnie and Arran sat in the front with Emily and me, James and Arran sat in the back. We were extremely tiered. We continued to talk a little bit longer and ate the boiled eggs and drank the milk we had left over. I was the last one to fall asleep. I couldn't. I had to remember. Something happened there. Something, important. I couldn't put my finger on it. It was annoying but eventually I drifted into the friendly embrace of sleep. That night I didn't have any bad dreams. It was the morning that I did. I woke up with a start. "guys, I know what happened at the hospital."

CHAPTER 9: SEPTEMBER 30TH, 2018

I opened the back doors and ran towards the front. I opened the doors as quick as I could. Ronnie woke up with a start. "Morning." He groaned. Emily lifted her head of the dashboard and scowled at me. As for Dylan, he stayed asleep. I paused for a second, slightly embarrassed. "I remember what happened at the hospital!" I exclaimed. "Give me 5 minutes." Said Emily resting her head on the dashboard again. "No! I need to tell you now!" I could hear swearing from the back as Arran woke up. Ronnie starred at me. And then my watch. "God sake mate it's like 6:30!" He replied and laid back down. I didn't have time for this. I honked the horn on the steering wheel and the three sat bolt upright. "Alright alright!" Said Emily. "Just give me a sec." I realised that we were on the small gravel road near our school. I went and sat down at the side, breathing in the cold early morning air. "What was that for!" Screamed Arran. I turned around. Arran was standing their bare foot looking like he just got dragged through a hedge backwards. I stood up and Looked directly at him. "I remember what happened at the hospital." I repeated for the third and then. "Jeez Arran take a mint." He shrugged and walked into the back of the van again and slammed the door. They took a long time to eventually get up and when they did they still looked like they were half asleep. They stumbled out of the van and walked over to me. I hesitated for a second. "Well..." I began. "This may take a little while." I sat there explaining all the details to them. By the end everyone looked concerned. "So your saying that a creepy person who you think is the organisation started to talk to you about his evil plan." Said Dylan. "Basically..." I replied. "Yeah." "This is bad, very bad." Said James. No one else replied. they looked too tired and shocked. "So he controls the cranks?" Asked James. I nodded. I looked about, half expecting there to be a massive crowd of cranks. I was wrong. What I got was an over statement. A whole army of cranks appeared to the left of us. They looked like they had been dragged out of bed early too. "Run!" I screamed. We all ran to the van. Ronnie sat in the front with Emily at the wheel and Me, Arran, James and Dylan stood in the back. Dylan slammed the doors. "This'll be fun." Said Arran. I rushed over to the bags and pulled out one of my toy sling shots that was way too powerful to be a toy. I did a bit more rummaging and found some rocks. The car backed down the driveway and down the road in a random direction. I kicked open the doors accompanied by moaning from the three. I took aim with my sling shot and loaded it with a rock. The cranks were crawling over each other in a chase to reach the van first. One of them was getting particularly close. An athletic 7-year-old was gaining on us. I took my aim and fired at it. I hit her in between the eyes and sent her flying backwards into the army of cranks. "I can't get all of them with a slingshot!" I shouted. "Then get them with this!" Shouted James and threw me one of the wooden boards. I threw it at the army and got a few of them. Every second they were gaining on us. Dylan stood with me and threw the other board at the army. He only got a few and was ultimately ineffective. "Great." He said. I looked about. Everyone looked deep in thought, the cranks getting further every second. I rushed over to the bag and took everything out of it but was cut off by the car swinging from side to side. I fell at the van wall along with Arran James and Dylan. "What!" Screamed James being thrown around the place. The doors were swinging everywhere and were even knocking out one or two cranks. I reached for the bag again and tipped everything out. "HELP!" Yelled Arran from the front of the van. A crank had grabbed a hold of his leg and was trying to pull him outside. I threw the bag at the crank and it slipped out the back, hand still on Arrans leg. James lunged forward and grabbed Arran's back before he became his very own crank mix. Arran wasn't light by the look of pain on James's face. I grabbed James's back and started to pull too, the doors still swinging about the place. Nothing too dramatic, just a bruise or too and a shout from Arran. The crank wasn't showing any signs of letting go. "Why not?" Said Dylan and grabbed my back. The crank let go and fell into the army behind him. We hauled Arran into the van. He stood up and brushed his shoulders. "Well that was"- DONG. I looked around. James was on the floor a massive bruise on his forehead. I ran over. "Out cold." I proclaimed. "That is one vicious door..." Said Dylan. With the help of Dylan I dragged James into the back of the van. "Now, about the bigger problem..." Said Arran. The population of the crank army had decreased but not by a lot. The van was still furiously rocking from side to side. "Oi, what the hell's going on up there?" I said. "A lot more than what's going on up there!" Ronnie replied. "Um, we can't exactly see..." Said Dylan. I heard a groan from Emily and didn't have to see to know that she was rolling her eyes. The cranks were advancing to the van. "What do we do now? We are literally out of supplies." Said Arran. I looked about. It was true. "I say we try and shake the cranks off and then find a place to stake this out." I said. I could hear Emily in the front saying something along the lines of yes master as we started to move towards the housing estate. The cranks were still on our tails. "We could always chuck Ronnie out the door?" Said Dylan. "I heard that!" Said Ronnie at the front. We were just turning into the place when. "What?" Said Emily. I leaned out the door and saw 2 cars outside, each with a middle-aged man on top with some form of weapon. They were screaming. "Well this day keeps getting more understandable." Said Arran. They started firing at the cranks with rocks and just about anything that you can think of. "What the hell is going on?" Said Dylan. I just kept on watching. The van continued to skid down the road lead by a smaller car with yet another slightly overweight middle-aged man on top. The cranks following us had dropped to 1. They lead us to a house that looked like dad had taken DIY to an extreme. "Move move move!" The man shouted trying not to smile. I could tell he was secretly enjoying this I jumped out the van as it was parking up and took everything in for a second. I looked at the van and saw Arran and Dylan dragging James out the back. I rushed over to help. The middle-aged man accompanied by what was probably his wife held the door open for us as Ronnie and Emily climbed out the front. The building was like all the other buildings apart from it was the biggest one there and most of it was boarded up with wood and metal. The post box I noticed, had a blade mechanism installed into is so a person behind could stab any unwanted visitors. God the fun I could've had with something like that at my house. We all piled through the door and were instantly met by a huge group of people. The best way to describe it is like someone brought a zombie to choir practice. There were mostly fathers and mothers in there with small children. I could see a few teenagers in amongst the crowd who looked tired. The man closed the door behind us. We looked around for familiar faces. Dylan's face lit up. "Mum! Dad!" He said.

CHAPTER 10: FAREWELL

Dylan ran over to his parents as we stood there and smiled. Me and Emily looked at each other and remembered our parents. I turned back and looked at the floor. They'll be fine. I thought. We had just found a bunch of survivors, so things must be going uphill a little bit. "A little bit of help would be appreciated!" Moaned Arran. I glanced behind me and saw him and Ronnie holding the body of an unconscious James. People started to shuffle out the way leading a clear path to the living room. Me, Emily, Ronnie and Arran all pilled in there dragging James along with us. We laid him on the large sofa and sighed as we stepped back and thought of what to do next. The living room was probably the most normal room in the whole house with only a few weapons dotted around the place. I sat down on the coffee table. "What do we do now?" Asked Ronnie. The man walked into the room with us slowly and looked like he was going to give a lecture about something. He sat on the sofa. It was clear by now that he was the leader of this relatively large group of people. "Our leader wants to see you." His exact same words were. I looked at the trio, they looked as confused as me. We shuffled through the crowd of people and was directed up the stairs. One by one we climbed the creaking steps and gazed at the hall decorations. The stairs were fairly small and there were a few smashed portraits of a happy family here and there. I sighed and stepped onto the landing. "Just over there." Said the man, pointing at one of the rooms. There was no one up here which probably explains why there were so many people downstairs. "Well I ain't going first." said Dylan who must've followed us. Arran stepped in and turned the doorknob. The door swung open and we were met by the sight of a room filled with weapons a desk and spiny chair. The chair had its back to us we all paused. "Hi…" I said. A second later the chair turned around slowly. We would have gasped but the whole thing was too absurd to do so. Sitting there was my maths teacher, Mr Bills. Emily tried not to laugh. It was like someone had replaced Dr.Claw from inspector gadget with a less then ominous maths teacher. "I have so many questions right now." Said Dylan. "Well that brings us to the topic of today." Mr. Bills said observing us. He beckoned us over and we all fought for the two chairs in front of his desk. Emily and Arran got the chairs and me Dylan and Ronnie had to stand. "So, we get ultimately captured by people who look like the character from mad max got a wife and kids and then confronted by our maths teacher." Said Dylan. He paused. It was true. "You must have a lot of questions right now." Mr. Bills replied. "Which is why I brought you here." He continued. We all fell silent. None of us had questions that weren't already obvious. "I'm." He began. "Mr. Bills." We all said cutting him off. He looked taken aback. "Well… Um… No one here actually knows who I am or was…" He said Facade gone. He looked sheepish. "Everyone else thinks that I was trained in the army… They call me big Dave…" He looked extremely embarrassed. "Well in that case, nice to see you again, just unfortunately under these circumstances. Never thought I'd see you again." He said. I wasn't listening. How did all these people get here?" I asked. I thought for a second. "Oh, yeah." He said. "It all started when I woke up in my maths chair. No one was there. I started to walk around. I found only a few people there who looked dead or knocked out. I left them because… Well… I don't know but I wanted to get away from that place any way. My next logical move was to go to the housing estate and work from there. And then we get here. I spotted a few people dotted around the place and decided to help them out. There were only a couple at first but as time went on more and more people started to appear, so I created this… Rebellion. I don't exactly know how all the zombies turned back to normal, but their stories were all the same. They all woke up after eating a lot of food. Infact, I think that too much of the poison cancels itself out!" I finished like it was a grand speech. I looked at our group. "Well if you want to call them zombies..." Said Arran. I sighed. "We have a lot to tell you." I said. We all walked out the door and were stopped. "I request you stay on campus, for safety of course." He said. We all nodded even though we had no intentions of staying here. We closed the door behind us. I looked at my watch, it was 6:30. We all walked down the stairs people shuffling out the way for us and into the living room. James was still asleep on the sofa, so we had to sit on the smaller one next to it. The people were just sort of sitting there, not really doing anything. I started to whisper to the others. "I say we make our move as soon as everyone is asleep, I doubt anyone will let a bunch of kids leave a safehold in the middle of an apocalypse." I said. Everyone nodded. It had been a few hours and we had explored around the whole house, including the storage cupboard where we had found all sorts of things, including these strange needles full of greenish brown liquid. I decided to only take a crossbow, a small knife and two walkie talkies. We told the man it was just in case, but I don't think he was fooled by that. We sorted out the walkie talkies. Then night came. We all lay on the floor, waiting for the last person to fall asleep. I looked at my watch. It was midnight. My greatest concern was how to get James in the van. Eventually they took a big yawn and lay down on the floor. I woke Ronnie, Emily, Arran and Dylan up even though it was clear they were all awake. We walked towards the door. It opened with barley any noise. I looked back and saw the four dragging James off the sofa and out of the living room. We all stepped out the door and I opened the back of the van for them everyone was prepping for the departure apart from Dylan. I looked at him. "Are you ok?" I asked. He scratched the back of his neck and looked at me. "Well I'm afraid this part of the journey you're going to have to take without me." He said. Everything stopped. I looked at him. "I've found my parents now; I can't lose them again." He said. I nodded. "Yeah..." I said, face falling. "Bye kid." Said James. He smiled. "You know." He started. "Ever since I met you on that dog walking route I have had the time of my life. I want to thank you for that." He was trying not to cry. I could tell. I jumped into the van and saluted at him. He saluted back. I was trying to smile. The van backed out the driveway and I watched as Dylan got further and further away. We turned a corner and I closed the doors and sat down on the van floor.

CHAPTER 11: THE BEGINNING OF THE END OF THE BEGINNING

I sat on the floor in the back of the van looking at the ground. The atmosphere was quiet, the complete opposite to the previous events. We had only lost one person, but the place was already much darker. "Where do we go now?" Asked Ronnie from the front. I Sighed. "I say we go to the alcove and wait for James to wake up." Said Arran. "Ryan?" Asked Emily. "I agree with Arran." I said. I heard the car boot up and back out of the estate and in a matter of seconds we were trundling down the road dogging cranks. I glanced at Arran he was trying to smile. The journey was pretty short, stopping at the end of the dog walking route. I opened the doors and helped Arran to drag James out the car. "We'll take turns carrying James ok?" Said Emily realising that James wasn't the lightest of people. After a good ten minutes we managed to jump over the barrier and into the woods. We only had to walk a bit more to get there but eventually we found it in the exact same state we left it. I slid down the hill and laid James on the ground. We all took a seat on the muddy floor and sat in silence. There was nothing we could do. The population of cranks were increasing, and the path looked murky and only went downhill. Ronnie arrived a bit later lugging all of the stuff in a bag. He sat down and looked at all of us. "Why the long faces?" He asked.

We shrugged. "Let's get an early night." I said. They nodded, and all laid down to sleep. I woke up with a start. I pinched myself. I wasn't dreaming. It was early morning and my clothes were caked in mud. "You awake yet James?" I whispered. No reply. I looked at the spot that we laid James. Wrong spot I thought. I sat up and looked round the alcove. I started to panic. He wasn't there. I stood up and woke the others up. "Not now..." Groaned Emily I turned on the spot. James was nowhere to be seen. "What's going on?" Asked Ronnie. There was a note nailed to a tree. I walked up to it and ripped it off the tree. Ryan goes alone or James dies. I looked into the distance. "Ryan?" Said Arran. I pocketed the note and grabbed a walkie talkie crossbow and a can of food. No one can track me with that. I ran up the hill and ran down the mud path. I leapt over the barrier and down the route. I glanced behind me. No one was following me. Good. I ran as fast I could. There were a few cranks about, but they were all a good distance away. I eventually found the van and jumped in the front and turned the keys. "Sneaky." I said. I knew what the organisation was doing. I stuck my middle finger up at the nearest CCTV camera and made my way to the hospital. I felt sorry for my friends, but this was all to save a life and that is our main priority. Here I was. The car was still there on the steps. I parked the car up and stepped out the door. I grabbed my crossbow and put my walkie talkie around my neck. I sighed and walked up the steps. I had to be brave. This was my fault and I would get everyone out of this situation. I kicked open the doors. The place was silent and empty. I spat on the floor and walked over to the elevator doors. I pressed the button to the top floor and stepped in. The doors closed, and I got my crossbow ready. The doors opened slowly. No one was there. "WHERE ARE YOU? WIMP!" I yelled. There was a pause. I was breathing heavy. "I thought we should meet in person." A voice said. I looked around. The smashed T.V was static. I aimed my crossbow I turned 360 degrees on the spot. There was the sound of footsteps by the corner at the end of the corridor. "YOU STAY AWAY FROM MY FRIENDS!" I yelled. The voice laughed. My finger was pressing against the trigger. The laughing was getting closer. And closer and then. I lanky man stood at the corridor. He was wearing a leather jacket and his face was covered by a bandana and sunglasses. I stepped back. He was just a small man. I felt scarred but also confused. "HA!" I shouted. "You're just a midget loser!" He stood there like a wall. I took my aim at him. "You win." He said. I just stood there and laughed. "What?" I said. "You win." He said again. I was angry. How dare he? HOW DARE HE! "I give up. My plan didn't work." He said. His calmness only made me angrier. I lowered my crossbow. "You have found the flaw to my plan. And for that I congratulate you. You win." He replied. I stared at him. "Where's James." I said. He still stood there. "He doesn't matter." He said. "Why are you doing this?" I said. "For fun. None of this required much skill. I just wanted to see your reaction. It was very amusing." He replied. I repeated. "Where's James." He lunged forwards. "He doesn't matter! He didn't do anything! It was you! You're the hero! Not him." He sounded angry. I picked my crossbow up and aimed it at his head. "You keep your distance if you don't want this in your skull! Now Where's James!" I yelled. He laughed. "Clever wasn't it? A perfect superhero movie. Do you like my plan? Bringing you here? No one will follow you! Genius!" I was confused and scared. "You had your chance. Now you die." I said. I pointed the crossbow at him. His façade was gone. "Shoot me." He said. I paused. I was angry scared and confused. "Shoot me." He repeated. I took my aim. I tried to pull the trigger. I couldn't. I screamed, face going red. He just stood there arms out wide. I pulled myself together and pulled the trigger. The shot fired and hit him in the chest. He slumped on the floor. I ran over to him. "Where's James!" I said looking at him. He laughed a spluttered. "The perfect ending." He said. His breathing slowed down almost a stop. I looked around and stood up. BANG. I was hit against the wall by a figure hard. A window smashed. I looked at the figure. It was James. I was rooted to the spot. He glanced at me briefly before jumping out the broken window. The man spluttered. "He's not bothered with you yet." He rasped. "He's going to your school to pick your friend Scott up." He spluttered. The man closed his eyes slowly and descended to hell. I pressed the button on my walkie talkie and gasped. "Go to the school, now!" I said slumping to the blooded floor. I tried to keep myself from passing out. I smacked myself and stood up. I stumbled towards the lift doors and pressed the button. The doors opened, and I stepped in, using the walls as support. I smacked myself some more and jumped out at the ground floor. I stumbled over to the doors and opened them. To the van. I thought. To the van. I tripped down the steps and towards the van. I opened the door and turned the ignition. This was not where my story ends.

CHAPTER 12: OCTOBER 1ST, 2018

I drove down the road swerving drastically. I couldn't concentrate. There was too much going on. I groaned, James is either a crank or dead, I wasn't too sure. If I were to get to the school from here it would be not too short. I had only gone a short distance when I saw a huge crowd of cranks. I swerved to a side expecting a fight, but they just kept on walking. They were going in the same direction as me and didn't seem to care about me that much. I frowned and wondered if I would make it before James. I aligned myself back up and continued to drive dodging the cranks. The drive was relatively straight forward and took only a few minutes to get there. I pulled up a hill and into the school's car park. I parked up and leapt out the van onto the tarmac. The place was deserted, and it felt eerie. I grabbed my crossbow and loaded it with an arrow. I had an intention of killing someone, but you never know. Emily Arran and Ronnie weren't here yet so I stumbled towards the back entrance. I opened the smashed glass door and walked slowly into the small area in between the sports hall and one of the buildings we called link. I walked straight through that area and outside. I had barely any supplies so I needed to be careful. I walked up the small steps and down a gravel path. I looked about. The buildings looked dilapidated and broken. The speakers were blurting out some pop song that sounded like a broken record. It was nothing short of ear-splitting. The fire had gone and left a gaping hole in one of the buildings. This is where it started and this is where I would end it. There were several grassy hills in between the gravel paths. It was a complete waste of space but no one really minded. At that moment Arran Ronnie and Emily burst in through the door behind me. I turned around lifting my cross bow. They raised their hands. "Jesus sorry!" Said Ronnie. I sighed. "Oh, it's you." I said dropping my weapon. They walked up to me panting. "Yo Ryan, we saw loads of cranks on the way up here, they didn't attack us just kept on walking!" Said Emily. I scoffed. Usually we would be happy that something like this happened. It was ever so slightly ironic. "Where the hell were you anyway?" Said Arran. I sighed. "Well... I woke up and couldn't find James and that was when saw a note saying that Ryan goes alone or James dies. I automatically knew where they wanted me to go so I hopped in the van and drove to the hospital." I looked at them. I was obviously going too fast. "Jeez I need to put this in a book." I said. I went on with the story. By the end they all looked shocked and confused. "C'mon we don't have much time and I have a plan." Said Arran breaking the silence. He then went on to explain a very complicated way of putting the anti-crank mix into the school sprinklers. "Then." He continued. "We start a small controlled fire so they go off and get the cranks to go under them. Sound good?" He said. We all nodded. Arran beaconed Ronnie towards one of the buildings. I turned to Emily. "So James is a crank?" Said Emily. I paused. "More of a... Super crank." I said. "I'm not sure what that psychopath gave him but it wasn't good." I concluded. "I suggest we grab weapons and call Dylan." Said Emily. I agreed. "Follow me." I said and walked over to the burnt buildings. I pushed open the door and ran up the stairs. I turned to the right to find The head's office. I pushed open the door. The place was extremely smashed up with notes everywhere and cabinets upturned. I rummaged around. "Here we go!" I exclaimed. Ages ago someone came into school with a sling shot that turned out to be extremely powerful. "So that's where that thing went!" Said Emily. I stood up admiring my handywork. "Won't we need more then that though..." Said Emily. I thought for a second.

"Well there are some cricket bats in the P.E sheds along with some javelins..." I said and with that Emily was off. I trudged out of her office and thought of what to do. Then I remembered. I grabbed my walkie talkie. I pressed the button. "Can you call Dylan please?" I said. I heard Arran talking to Ronnie. "Calling him now." Said Arran the sound of Hammering in the background. I put the walkie talkie down and ran down the corridor. There were several science classrooms down here, only one of them wasn't burnt to the ground. I stopped in my tracks. "Great." I said. I could see the classroom, there was just a massive hole in the way. "Well how do I get there then..." I said. The hole was 5 meters long and impossible to jump. I was planning to use the Bunsen burners from there and set something on fire that way but alas. I grabbed my hair and thought some more. I don't have time for this. Maybe we could smash the computers downstairs? I didn't have any other ideas so I ran back the other way and towards the stairs. I rushed down them and almost tripped. I opened another door to the downstairs of the building and took the arrow out of my crossbow. I wouldn't need it. I walked over to the computers in the middle of the room and smashed one with my crossbow. A small fire started out. "I'm going to need more then that!" I said and hit another one. And another. I smiled. This was sort of fun. A bonfire started in the place and I ran out the way and looked at it. It was just enough smoke to set the sprinklers off alright. I picked up my walkie talkie. "We have a fire." I said into it. "Thanks but we're a bit busy at the moment." Said Arran the other end. I put it down and starred in horror as the fire started to grow even more. I ran out the nearest fire exit and into the open space. I heard the sound of yelling from a few meters away. I looked about wildly and then Emily burst through the door leading to the link a little way away. She was running towards me. "What's up?" I said. She stumbled up to me breathing heavy. She took a deep breath. "The cranks...They're here but they're just sort of standing there." I looked at her. "Show me." I said. We ran down the steps and pushed open the doors to the link. We ran to the end of it and opened the smashed door. I was taken aback. "Whoa!" I said.

There was a line of cranks around the school. All standing there. They weren't even laughing. Just, standing there. I walked up to one slowly. I hit it. It didn't move at all. I wouldn't have minded much if they weren't making it completely impossible for anyone to get in or out. My walkie talkie beeped. I picked it up. "Yes?" I said. "The cranks have arrived but they're not moving much. Like at all." Ronnie said. "Same here." Said Emily. I turned it off and looked at Emily. "Any weapons?" I said. She passed me a wooden cricket bat. I swung it about a bit. "This should do it." I said and walked back into link followed by Emily. "Should we attack the cranks? I mean what is there goal?" I thought for a second pushing open the door. "We'll leave them there for a moment." I said to her walking up the steps. I looked across the open space. My walkie talkie beeped again. I picked it up. "Man down!" Arran shouted. "What?" I replied. "Watch out, He's coming for you!" Arran said before turning it off. Emily looked about warily. Then I saw him. His clothes were ripped, cuts all the way down his body. I slowly looked upwards until my eyes met his face his teeth were jagged, his eyes a sickly milky white, with greenish white pupils, staring at me with a grin on his twisted face. I starred in horror as the monster that once was James ran straight at us.

CHAPTER 13: WAR

I stood there rooted to the spot watching as James was running straight at me. He was getting closer and closer and then SMACK. He hit me right in the stomach sending me flying some 3 meters away. I fell against the railing wincing. It looked like James was ready to hit me again. I groaned. He was inches away when. "TAKE THIS!" Screamed Emily and hit James with the wooden bat I the head. He stopped in his tracks, dead still for a second. He looked up at me, wiping blood from his mouth and ran at me. I dived to a side and ran over to one of the grass hills and took cover. James looked puzzled. He turned about on the spot, looking for us. I looked through terrified eyes at Emily. James started walking over to a drainpipe and ripping it straight off the wall he growled, his search light like eyes searching us out. I gripped my cricket bat tight. I glanced at my walkie talkie and hoped that Arran and would be done soon. Then he saw us. James ran over to us, drainpipe in hand. I picked Emily up and we ran some way into the nearest building. I was faster at running than James and by the looks of things Emily as well. He was still following us. "In here!" Shouted Arran from somewhere. I looked around and saw him holding a door open. We rushed in there. There was mad scramble and a lot of shouting as we closed the door on James just in time. We were in a classroom, a small one but still a classroom none the less. "Any progress?" I said. Arran nodded. "We've been set back a bit though, Ronnie got attacked and isn't in a good state, follow me." We went with Arran into a small room next to it. Ronnie was lying there, the stiches on his face cut loose revealing a horrible gash down his face. Emily winced. I walked over to Ronnie and checked his temperature. "He's boiling!" I said. "Quick, we need a wet cloth, anything!" The two ran off and the banging at the door got considerably louder. "Thanks James." Ronnie muttered. Arran and Emily arrived shortly after with a cloth. I dabbed it on Ronnie's forehead. He groaned some more. I stood up and joined Arran and Emily. I glanced at Arran. "How long are you going to be?" I said to Arran. He shrugged. "An hour?" He replied. I heard smashing behind me. I spun around. James was standing there, a massive hole in the chunky fire door, his fist bleeding. I stepped back. "Grab your bat." I said to Emily. I raised my cricket bat, running at the door and opened it, sending James flying backwards. I stopped for a minute. "RUN!" I said and me and Emily ran out the door and behind one of the hills. I heard gunshots and smiled. The survivors were here. Only now did I realise the sheer size of their army. Loads of them started to dive over the wall, flaming torches drills and an Arrangement of B&Q items in hand. There were a decent amount of them, enough to take down James with ease. The crowd of survivors shuffled to aside and Mr. Bills walked to the front of the crowd with a shot gun and a leather jacket. I grinned. James snarled, setting his blank eyes upon them. He backed up to the wall. Mr. Bills looked at him and promptly said. "Tie him down." To a group of burly men. They walked over to him, panic in James's eyes. He stood there for a minute before starting to laugh. The men were undeterred and kept walking. James kept on laughing. I frowned and looked at Emily. I could tell Mr. Bills was confused behind his sunglasses. I little way away I heard another person laughing. And another. My heart skipped a beat. The crank army. Everyone fell silent and even the burly men stopped. My walkie talkie beeped but I didn't pick it up. The laughing got louder and louder. A window smashed. I looked about in shock. There was the sound of stumbling from the entrance building and a small teenage girl appeared out of one of the doors. Another window smashed, and another, and another. I watched in horror as more and more cranks started to file into the open space. Mr.

Bills stepped back. The laughing got louder and louder until there was at least 150 cranks in the open space. It got louder and louder and then stopped. The air was silent. I wasn't breathing. The burly men had backed off and I hoped to god that Arran and Ronnie were ok. A crank wailed and ran at the group. Then the whole army. BANG BANG BANG. I could hear Mr. Bills's gun going off and numerous other weapons. It was pandemonium. Cranks were flying everywhere and there was a lot of shouting. I stood up. Where was James? I looked at Emily. She was as pale as a sheet. I was about to make my way into one of the buildings when a red-faced boy made his way out of the conundrum. I squinted at him. Is it... Dylan? He came running up to us. Emily looked even more shocked. "Hey guys!" He said. I looked at him. He had my sling shot and a small revolver in his pocket. I smiled at him. The team was back together again. I remembered. Now was not the time. "Come on." I said. "I think I know where James will be." We ran towards the small area that we used to sit at lunch. This was the last place that things were normal. We ran over the mounds and I pushed open the fire door and under the large set of stairs. We all stood there, looking around. I frowned. I could hear growling. Somewhere. "Is it true that James is a crank?" Asked Dylan. I didn't reply. Something, was wrong. "Oh God..." Said Emily. She was looking up. James was on the ceiling. No. He was literally on the ceiling. "What the hell!" I said. I snarled and leapt down 2 stories. We all dispersed to the sides. This wasn't going to be easy. With the other cranks they were easy to take down, but I didn't know what that man gave him. I raised by bat as he stood up in the middle of the room, starring at us all, a demonic expression on his face. I lunged forward and kicked him in the stomach weak enough not to do any long-term damage. He stepped back but was otherwise undeterred. He immediately took a step towards me and pinned me against the wall in a second. I could hear Emily and Dylan yelling as I floated there by the neck. I spluttered. I could see Emily and Dylan hitting James but nothing worked. I choked and kneed him in the side. He grunted and I could see his blank eyes twitching for a second. My vision fuzzed and my breath shallowed. I could still faintly hear the two in the background. James dropped me and ran out of the door beside us. I fell on the floor gasping. Emily and Dylan ran over to me. "What was that about?" Asked Emily. I shrugged, panting. "Go after him Dylan!" I gasped. He stood up and chased after James. I glanced out the window. The battle didn't show any signs of stopping. A bang came from the restaurant next to us. I stood up and followed Dylan who looked like he was going to the library. My bat now felt heavy in my hand like a weight. I was suddenly stopped in my tracks. It was the mad farmer. I hit him in the face. I backed off but unexpectedly came back. Emily had my back. She hit him with the bat in the stomach and he fell on the floor. I sighed and looked around I had lost all trace of Dylan and James. I growled. I looked at Emily. She had a scar on her arm. The most damage I had taken was James almost cutting my lip. I looked around some more. "Great." Said Emily. I heard shouting from upstairs. It sounded like Dylan. Me and Emily made our way over to the closest set of stairs and ran up them. There was no sign of them. At all. Another shout came. It was from my English classroom. I turned left and ran a little way down the corridor towards probably the largest classroom in the school. I opened the doors. And saw Dylan and James there fighting each other. Chairs and tables were up turned and I could see the cupboard open with books falling out of it. I ran over and hit James with my bat in the arm. He shrieked and stumbled back tripping over a table. Emily ran at him and was ready for another hit when James grabbed the bat and quite literally swung her out the way. She hit several chairs and a table before slumping over a desk. I gasped and looked at James. "You're going to pay for that." I said to him. I ran at him and raised my club. I hit him with the end of my bat square in the face. I fell on the floor behind him and watched as he fell over clutching his head. "Ryan!" Shouted Dylan. "He's still our friend!" He said. He was right. I dropped my bat and ran over to James. I noticed that Emily was up and walking with a dazed expression on her face. I stood over James. The air was silent apart from the sound of gun shots and shouting from the survivors outside. I don't know exactly what happened next but in short James threw us all back and smashed through the window with a table. We sat there, all stunned. Dylan was coughing and we were all fairly battered. I leapt over to the window in time to see James disappear into the conundrum of the battle. I saw cranks and humans lying everywhere across the place and weapons in every inch of the space. No body looked dead which was the only good thing in this situation. My walkie talkie beeped. I picked it up, going to help the others to get up. It was Arran. "How's Ronnie?" I asked. There was a long pause as I lifted Emily off the ground. "He's ok." Arran replied. "Any way, I need food, a lot of it." He said. There was a stop and what sounded like Arran fighting something off. I noticed that all three of us were badly injured. Arran returned to his device. "How are you that end?" Asked Arran. "Tired, angry." Said Emily. I sighed looking out the window. "James got away." I said. "He's gone into the crowd." Arran hammered something. "Any way, where do you want it?" I asked. "Directly below you, in the classroom we were just in." Said Arran. I turned the walkie talkie off and walked over to the classroom entrance. "We'll go to the restaurant, there should be food left there." I said. They nodded wearily. Dogging tables and chairs, I made my way towards the doors and heaved them open. I looked behind me. The others were stumbling along with me. On good sign. I ran down the battered corridor and opened another set of doors that led us to the restaurant. I stared at the farmer laying on the ground twitching like a squashed fly. "Down here!" I shouted and ran down a small flight of steps. Next to me was the table that we sometimes used to sit at break. Images flashed through my mind. We were happy. Me, Ronnie, Scott, Arran and James. All sitting there, oblivious to the darkness that was later to envelop our lives. I remembered the task in hand and rushed to the counter at the end of the hall where they served food. I jumped over the counter and waited for Emily and Dylan. A few seconds later they hobbled over the counter and joined me. I spotted the fridges in the corner. "Over there!" I said to the group. They nodded and we all walked over to the fridges and pulled them open and took out as much food as we could hold. Food pouring out of our hands we jumped back over the counter and towards the rendezvous location. I kicked open the door and we all dropped the food into a pile. Arran was hammering in a small hole he had made in the floor, taking out pipes. "Here it is." I said. He stopped and stood up. "Great!" He replied, pushing it in the direction of the hole. "All I need to do now is put this in there and press the button in the room next door!" I looked at him, panting. "I'll go get the survivors to lure the cranks under the sprinklers then." I said. I ran over to the end of the room and opened the smashed fire door. "I'm coming too." Said a voice. We all looked round. Ronnie was standing there; stiches open on his face revealing a massive gash down his face. I grimaced at the sight. I glanced at Emily. "Well we need all the people we can get..." She said. I paused and the nodded at him. We walked out the doors and were instantly met by a crank flying past us. I stepped back, alarmed. I cautiously moved further into the open space, or what was the open space. There were people everywhere and weapons all across the place. It was nothing short of pandemonium. I could see Mr. Bills at the side, fighting of hordes of cranks. I didn't have any weapons. Great. I turned back. "Ready?" I said. They nodded. "I'll going to talk to Mr. Bills, you guys help the other survivors." And with that we ran into the heat of the battle. I dived and ducked out the way of cranks humans and generally any object left up for grabs. It looked like we were winning, but it might not stay that way. Mr. Bills looked like he was having the time of his life. He wasn't actually using his shot gun, more using it as a warning. Watch out, maths teacher with a strictly illegal weapon. He was battering cranks left right and centre, only occasionally stopping to align his broken sunglasses. I called out to him and saw the confusion on his face as he looked around. The sound of a gun went off as an over enthusiastic crank shot a bullet into the air in the middle of the place. He dived behind a mound and I saw my chance. I ran over to him, skidding down the gravel path. I threw myself against the hill to his surprise. I lay there for a moment, catching my breath and listening to the sound of guns and shouting. "I need your help." I said. There was a pause as Mr. Bills added a new round to his shot gun. He sighed. "What now?" He asked. "I need your help to get the cranks inside the building." I replied. He scoffed and looked at me. "What's that going to do?" He questioned. I sighed in annoyance. "Are you still holding a grudge against me for leaving your 'Rebellion'? This is a war; we can't afford this!" I said a little too loudly." He scowled at me before jumping up and skidding down the hill to re-join the fight. I heard a growling noise. I looked about. At the end of the gravel path there were two boys. I looked at them more. "Oh no." They were the two boys that beat us up under the stairs and the first cranks were encountered. Great. I thought. I glanced about and saw a wrench lying on the floor. I walked over to it and picked it up. I swung it around a bit. "This should be easy." I said. A chill went down my spine. I looked behind me and saw the old man who's phone I had stolen standing there, drunk façade gone, replaced with a slightly more psychopathic one. I grimaced. "The more the merrier." I mumbled. I backed into the middle of the path. "Look, I'm sure we've had our misunderstandings but..." I started. My heart sank as I saw Scott walk up the hill and loom over me. His face looked burnt and his skin thoroughly irritated and red. I gulped. He looked furious. "Oh god!" I managed to say before he ran at me. I ducked his punch and jabbed him in the ribs with the wrench. He yelled and I backed off clutching my ears. "Gut wrenching." I mumbled to myself. Scott came back and hit me in the face. I clutched my jaw in pain and kicked him in the knee he buckled down and I spat blood on the floor and watched in horror as the old man and the two boys started to run at me, the boys considerably faster than the old man. I legged it over a mound and behind a metal bench. They were still following me. I stood on the bench. The boys were getting closer. And closer. BANG. I jumped down on one of them and hit them square on the head with the tool. I landed on the ground next to him and gave him a firm upper cut to the jaw and a knife hand to the stomach. I bent over and doubled back. I dashed behind him, kicked him in the back of the leg and threw him into the bench with a satisfying DONG. I had little time to appreciate the martial arts I had just done because seconds later the second boy wrapped a metal cord around my neck. I spluttered and choked. The old man was getting closer with every second. I back kicked him and landed it where I hoped it would be effective. It was. He bent back lost his balance and fell on the ground. I rolled aside, tearing the cord off my neck and standing up. I kicked him aside for good measure and braced myself for another attack. The old man was inches away, growling furiously. I swung my wrench as hard as I could at the old man and he was soon sent flying towards the ground. I sighed with relief. The I remembered. I grabbed the groaning man by the scruff of his neck and started dragging him to the nearest fire exit. I watched as he willingly let me drag him across the tarmac floor, half knocked out. To his dismay I dropped him on the ground and heaved open the fire door. I clutched his arm and dragged him over the threshold and into the building. I looked up. The computers were still burning contently in the middle. I left the man lying on the floor next to the fire and went to collect the two boys. I had barely stepped out the door when I was instantly thrown back. A flurry of red and orange filled the air as an ear-splitting BOOM sounded. I sat up and looked ahead of me, head spinning. I could hear shouting and gun fire. Sounded like a crank had got a hold of some explosives I stood up. "Oh God." I said. I ran over the mounds, dodging the conundrum of cranks and found the spot where it had gone off. Mr. Bills was lying there along with many other survivors and cranks alike. I walked over to him. He wasn't in a good state. He was groaning and mumbling something under his breath. I was pushed off as the middle-aged man that had saved us from the crank army came by. "Dave, you ok?" He said over his body. "What does it look like?" He mumbled. I could see Ronnie Dylan and Emily running over. The explosion had picked off a lot of the two armies, leaving only a handful of each still in combat. "I will command them from now on, I will lead us to victory!" The man said. "I ain't dead yet!" Mr. Bills said. Now was my chance. I pushed the man out the way to his discomfort and loomed over 'Big Dave'. "It's time to put our differences aside." I said to him. "We're outnumbered by them. You know that. You knew that all along." He grinned, a slightly annoyed expression. "What I'm trying to say is." I started. "I can get a hint kid." Mr. Bills reluctantly said clutching his wounded arm. I smiled smugly. "But...But...He left our camp! He's a traitor! You can't just do this!" The man said. Mr. Bills rolled his eyes and said. "Look mate, we're already screwed so why not give it a shot?" There was a long pause. I grinned and looked at the three. They grinned back. Mr. Bills rolled over groaning. The old man stood there for a second before looking straight at me. "What do we do now." He said croakily. "We have a plan." I said looking at the classroom Arran was in. "Everyone, take the cranks inside!" The man yelled at the rebels. There was a lot of heated discussion but eventually they started to grab the cranks and drag them towards the nearest building. I ran over to Emily Ronnie and Dylan. "Where's James?" I said. They all shrugged. I bit my fingernails. "He's probably ran off somewhere, anyway, we don't have time to deal with him." Emily said. "Right." I eventually said. "I'm going to call Arran." They nodded and dispersed. I walked over to a wall and pressed the button on the walkie talkie. A second later Arran picked up. "You ready yet?" I said. "Give me five minutes." He said. I swallowed. "Have you seen James?" I said. "No." Arran replied I sighed. "Call me if you do." I said and turned my walkie talkie off. I clapped my hands together and ran over to help a group of survivors trying to tackle down a particularly vicious crank. A few minutes later everything was in place. I closed the fire door behind me and waited. "What do we do now?" Asked the man. I looked at my watch. "Food should start coming down from the sprinklers any second now." I replied. I started tapping. Nothing. "What's going on?" Whispered Dylan. I pressed my walkie talkie. "What's going on down there?" I said into it. Silence. I dropped my walkie talkie. Out of the corner of my eye I could see a crank flinching. And another one. "Oh no." One of the survivors said. I pressed the button. "Any time today would be appreciated!" I yelled into it. Yet again no reply. One of them started growling. A chill went down my spine. The man looked at me. Someone grabbed my back. I turned around. On the end was a teenage boy

59

grinning at me. I hit it with my wrench. And noticed that the other cranks were starting to wake up. All of them were laughing. It's James. I thought. He's controlling them. I backed out the fire door behind me. "Where are you going?" Asked Ronnie. "Somethings wrong." I replied walking over the threshold, watching in terror as the cranks slowly started to rise up and fight. I ran towards the building that Arran was in as fast as I could. Something was terribly wrong. I burst open through the fire doors and looked around. The room was silent. Apart from the sound of laughing. It wasn't happy laughter. It was cold and shallow, like the cackle of a witch. I held my breath and glanced around the room, shaking. Good news, I found Arran. Bad news…He was slumped over a table with a missing finger. My eyes started to tear up. Look at where the three had got to now? I was hunting down one of my best friends that had just ripped a finger off our friend. "I know you're in here." I said, voice wobbling uncontrollably. Blood was seeping out of Arran finger. The laughing grew louder and louder. Then stopped. I whimpered. BANG I was thrown to the floor and next thing I knew James was on top of me snarling, his unforgiving eyes wild. I screamed, James's fingernails digging into my throat. I tried feebly to push him off. "It's me." I winced weakly. He seemed undeterred, crouching there, choking me. My vision was blurring. His expression weakened a bit. He leapt off me and into a corner. I sat up. "You know that. Under the stairs, you saw that, it's us! Please, wake up!" I said to him. The door behind me was open, revealing a massive electrical box with a red button on it. I crawled over there. I had to do it. I had only crawled a few inches away when I was dragged back. I rolled over to see James in front of me with a knife. "You don't want to do this." I whispered to him. He smiled widely; his eyes wild. He plunged the knife into my leg. I screamed. I tried not to look at the wound. I gulped, scrabbling for air. "Goodnight Ryan, this isn't a war, this is a revolution." Tears seeped out of my eyes. "I'm your friend, James, remember? The times you had with us. Remember the combine harvester? Remember?" I said, my eyes blurring with tears. The pain was unbearable. James shrieked and ran over to a wall. He smacked his head against it, screaming. I crawled over to the box slowly, using all the effort I had left. James snarled and turned to look at me, flinching. The fire door I had opened through suddenly opened. "What the hell is going on?" Emily Ronnie and Dylan were there in the doorway. James shrieked grabbing a chair. The three stumbled back. He stared at them. He threw the chair at the window and crouched at the window ledge. He took one last look at me and leapt out of the window and out of sight. I sat there for a second, soaking everything in. I swallowed and pressed the button. The three ran over to me, my eyes blurring, I heard shouting faintly as my hearing fuzzed. I slumped to the floor and embraced the darkness.

TO BE CONTINUED
IN WELCOME TO THE
APOCALYPSE BOOK 2,
FRIEND, A FOE, A FIRE

Printed in Great Britain
by Amazon